Pop Pop Pop!

Written by Catherine Baker
Illustrated by Beatriz Castro

Collins

Get a pot, Ted.

2

Set it up, Ted.

3

Tip it in, Ted.

4

Pop to the top.

6

Pop pop pop pop

7

Get a tin, Mum.

pop pop
pop pop

9

Pop up to the socks.

Pop up to the tum.

Ted gets Mum.

No, pot, no.

/e/

14

·10·

 After reading

Letters and Sounds: Phase 2

Word count: 50

Focus phonemes: /g/ /o/ ck /e/ /u/

Common exception words: to, the, go, no

Curriculum links: Maths: Space, shape and measures

Early learning goals: Listening and attention: listen to stories, accurately anticipating key events and respond to what is heard with relevant comments, questions or actions; Understanding: answer 'how' and 'why' questions about experiences and in response to stories or events; Reading: children use phonic knowledge to decode regular words and read them aloud accurately; they also read some common irregular words.

Developing fluency

- Go back and read the chant to your child, using lots of expression.
- Make sure that your child follows as you read.
- Pause so they can join in and read with you.
- Say the whole chant together. You can make up some actions to go with the words.

Get a pot, Ted.	Pop to the top.	Pop up to the socks.
Set it up, Ted.	Pop, pop, pop, pop.	Pop up to the tum.
Tip it in, Ted.	Get a tin, Mum,	Ted gets Mum.
Go pot, go pop.	Pop, pop, pop, pop.	No, pot, no.

Phonic practice

- Point to the word **get** on page 2. Model sounding it out 'g-e-t' and blending the sounds together **get**. Ask your child if they can find a word on page 3 that rhymes with **get** (*set*). Can they think of any other words that rhyme with **get** and **set**? (e.g. *jet, met, net*)
- Now look at the I spy sounds pages (14–15) together. Which words can your child find in the picture with the /e/ or /u/ sounds in them? (e.g. *letter, envelope, ten, eggs, elf, bell, brush, duck, umbrella, mugs*)